WOOF
FINDS A FAMILY

by Danae Dobson
Illustrated by Dee deRosa

WORD PUBLISHING
Dallas · London · Sydney · Singapore

I would like to dedicate this book to my dad, James Dobson.
Through the years he has been my very good friend,
a devoted father,
and one of the most interesting people I know.
I love you, Dad.

Woof Finds a Family
previously published as **Woof! A bedtime story about a dog**
Copyright ©1979, 1989 by Danae Dobson for the text. Copyright ©1989 by Dee deRosa for the illustrations.
All rights reserved. No portion of this book may be reproduced in any form without the written permission
of the publishers, except for brief quotations in reviews.
Scripture quotation is from *The Living Bible, Paraphrased,* copyright 1971 by Tyndale House Publishers,
Wheaton, IL. Used by permission.
Library of Congress Cataloging-in-Publication Data
Dobson, Danae.
Woof finds a family/by Danae Dobson: illustrated by Dee deRosa.
   p. cm.
Previously published as: Woof.
Summary: When a shaggy mutt saves the life of six-year-old Mark, the Petersons adopt the stray dog.
   ISBN 0-8499-8345-2:
   1. Children's writings, American. [1. Dogs — Fiction. 2. Children's writings.] I. DeRosa, Dee, ill. II. Title.
PZ7.D6614Ws 1989
[E] — dc20   89-16624
Printed in the United States of America   CIP
   01239RA9876543   AC

A MESSAGE FROM
Dr. James Dobson

Before you read about this dog named Woof perhaps you would like to know how these books came to be written. When my children, Danae and Ryan, were young, I often told them stories at bedtime. Many of those tales were about pet animals who were loved by people like those in our own family. Later, I created more stories while driving the children to school in our car pool. The kids began to fall in love with these pets, even though they existed only in our minds. I found out just how much they loved these animals when I made the mistake of telling them a story in which one of their favorite pets died. There were so many tears I had to bring him back to life!

These tales made a special impression on Danae. At the age of twelve, she decided to write her own book about her favorite animal, Woof, and see if Word Publishers would like to print it. She did, and they did, and in the process she became the youngest author in Word's history. Now, ten years later, Danae has written five more, totally new adventures with Woof and the Petersons. And she is still Word's youngest author!

Danae has discovered a talent God has given her, and it all started with our family spending time together, talking about a dog and the two children who loved him. We hope that not only will you enjoy Woof's adventures but that you and your family will enjoy the time spent reading them together. Perhaps you also will discover a talent God has given you.

It was a wet August day as Krissy and Mark Peterson looked out of Krissy's second-story bedroom window.

"Look at the rain come down," Mark said, peering down at the sidewalk. "What a day to splash in the puddles."

"Not now," Krissy replied. "I don't feel like it. Actually, I don't feel like doing anything."

"Me neither," Mark said, looking up at ten-year-old Krissy. "Let's just watch the rain."

As they sat at the window, a man in a black raincoat walked briskly down the sidewalk. Stumbling up to the man came a wet, shaggy-haired dog who looked like he hadn't had a bath in weeks. He rubbed his head against the man's pant leg, as if asking to be petted.

"Get away, mutt!" the man shouted and kicked the poor dog into the gutter. "Leave me alone!"

The dog lifted his head and watched the man round the corner of Maple Street.

"Krissy!" Mark said, grabbing her sleeve. "Did you see that?"

Instead of answering, Krissy ran down the stairs and out the door. Six-year-old Mark followed as fast as he could. Krissy picked up the dog affectionately, although he was almost too heavy for her to carry. The dog licked her hand gratefully. By the time Mark burst out the front door, Krissy was returning to the house.

"Let me hold him! Let me pet him!" Mark begged impatiently.

"Wait," Krissy replied, frowning at him.

Mrs. Peterson heard the commotion and came outside, holding a newspaper to shield her hair from the rain.

"Krissy, Mark," she shouted. "What on earth are you doing with that ugly, filthy dog?"

"Mom, this is our new pup," said Mark. "You can tell he doesn't belong to anyone. He doesn't even have a collar on. Please can we keep him?"

"Certainly not. You can get that idea out of your mind. I don't want to even discuss it. Now put him down and come in the house. Your clothes are soaked already."

But the children would not give up that easily.

"Mom," Mark said, "he doesn't have a home. Couldn't we just keep him until tomorrow? Please?"

Mrs. Peterson looked at the animal. Indeed he was a sight. He looked up at her with pitiful eyes and then wagged his crooked little tail. Mrs. Peterson's heart softened as she said, "Okay. You can keep him until this weekend. He does need a dry bed and some food."

"Oh boy!" both children shouted at the same time.

"Wait," Mrs. Peterson cautioned. "I said you could only keep the dog until Saturday night. Maybe we can find him a good home by then."

The two children raced toward the house with the animal beside them.

"Krissy," said Mrs. Peterson, "I don't want to be unkind, but I refuse to have that filthy dog in our house. You can make him a soft bed in the garage. And I suggest you give him a bath."

"All right. Come on, Mark," said Krissy. "Let's give him a bath. You go get a tub and some soap, and I'll get some old rags and towels."

When the children had everything ready, they set the dog in the tub of soapy water. They couldn't believe how dirty he was. At least a thousand fleas were scampering around his furry body.

"That's why he scratches all the time," said Krissy. "This poor dog must be miserable."

They scrubbed him until he was clean.

"Phew," Krissy said, wiping the sweat off her forehead. "That's done."

Then they dried him off and dusted him down with flea powder left over from the time they had taken care of the Smiths' cat. Mark found one of his old toothbrushes and brushed the dog's teeth, although the animal didn't seem to appreciate the favor.

"Finally," Krissy said when they finished. "Have you thought about what we're going to name him?"

"Not really," Mark said. "He looks like a Rover to me."

"No, that's too common," Krissy replied. "How about Penny?"

"No-o-o . . . Hey, let's ask <u>him</u> what he wants to be called," Mark said.

They both looked at the dog. As if he had read their minds, the dog barked WOOF.

"How about that?" said Krissy. "He answered us. I think Woof is a great name."

"Me too," Mark said. "Let's name him Woof."

At dinner that evening the children could talk to their father of nothing but Woof, and how they found him, and everything that had happened that day. They were still upset about the man in the raincoat who had kicked their pup.

As Mother was bringing the dessert, an awful thing happened. Woof managed to push open the door between the house and the garage. He bounded into the living room in the direction of his new friends. But as he was coming through the doorway, he slid on the hardwood floors and crashed into a tea table which held a vase. The vase toppled and fell to the floor, breaking into a million pieces. Mother shrieked and Father gasped.

Mrs. Peterson began to wail about the antique vase, which had been in the family for ninety years. Krissy ran to Woof and started to lead him back to the garage.

"Just look at that mess!" Mr. Peterson said. "Either you find a home for that animal by tomorrow afternoon or he is going to the pound!"

"No," Mark begged. "Please!"

But Mr. Peterson had made up his mind. He picked up the newspaper and sat down on the sofa. The two children ran up the stairs in tears. They both knew what the pound meant . . . *Death!*

That night when Mr. Peterson came upstairs to tell the children good-night, he found them saying their prayers. He stood around the corner as they asked God to help them. Krissy prayed first. "Dear Lord, please help the dog not to go to the pound. You made him, and you know that he doesn't have anybody to love him or take care of him. If Mother and Dad won't let us keep him, then please help us to find a warm home for him. The Bible says you care about little sparrows. So you must love our dog, too. Please take care of him. Amen."

When Krissy finished, Mark prayed, saying the same things his sister had said. After they had finished praying, they looked up to see their father standing over them. He put loving arms around his children and pulled them close to him. Then Mr. Peterson sat on the bed, with a child on each side.

"You know, children," he began, in his quiet, steady voice, "I once had an experience similar to this. We had a dog named Pal when I was a boy, and we had to give him away because we moved. I was sick about losing him, but I soon got over it. That's how it will be with you. I know you're upset now, but you'll feel better in a few days."

"But, Dad, your dog didn't have to go to the pound, did he?" asked Krissy.

"Well, no, we gave him to the people next door. But I don't know anyone in this neighborhood who wants a dog. And we can't keep every stray that wanders by here. Besides, this is the ugliest mutt I've ever seen. He has a crooked leg and one ear that flops over. He is just not the kind of dog that people want for a pet. That's why no one else has adopted him."

There was a long pause after Mr. Peterson had spoken, and it was obvious that he hadn't made the children feel any better. Mark wiped a tear from his left eye.

Finally their father spoke again. "If you really want a dog that much, I'll get you a German shepherd puppy. He'll be a thoroughbred you can be proud of. Okay?"

Krissy broke into tears. "But this dog needs us. He doesn't have a family," she cried.

"Now, don't worry about it anymore," Mr. Peterson said. "Just get some sleep, and you'll feel better in the morning." He kissed Mark and Krissy on their cheeks, tucked them in their beds and went downstairs.

Krissy drifted off to sleep in a matter of minutes, but she was restless and fitful. She dreamed that she and Mark were sitting in the pound watching the person who puts animals to sleep. He filled his needle with fluid and then

took their dog into the next room. Krissy heard the dog yelping from behind the closed door. Then the man began to laugh so loudly that she awoke in a cold sweat, sitting upright in bed.

Although Krissy tried to go back to sleep, she could not quit thinking about the dog. She tossed and turned for almost an hour. Finally she got up and slipped downstairs. All was quiet and dark. She thought she saw a figure floating near the wall, but it was only her shadow.

Krissy felt her way into the gloomy garage and looked around her. Then she heard the soft patter of feet coming toward her. It was Woof. She knelt beside him and stroked his rough fur. He snuggled up close to his new friend and licked her hand as if to say, "I know I'm not worth much. I know I'm ugly and I'm just a mutt. You did what you could, and I understand." Krissy couldn't bear it any longer. She gave him a last pat and went back to bed.

The next morning when Krissy and Mark woke up, they could hear the sound of bacon sizzling and eggs frying. They rushed to the kitchen just as Mother was pouring the orange juice.

"Good morning, children," she said cheerfully. "You're just in time for breakfast." Father had already begun eating and was reading the paper.

No one talked about the dog throughout the meal, but everybody was thinking about him. When they were through eating, Father pushed back his chair and said, "Well, I'd best be getting to work."

After saying the usual good-byes, he picked up his briefcase and gave Mother a kiss. As he was nearing the doorway, he said, "I'll be home at six o'clock to take care of the dog. You have him ready to go when I get home." He smiled. "Don't worry, kids. It's going to be all right." Then he left.

After Krissy and Mark cleared the table, Mrs. Peterson called the children to do some household chores. It was Krissy's turn to help with the vacuuming and Mark's to take out the garbage. He finished first, so he called Woof and they went outside.

"Come on, Woof," Mark said. "Let's see if we can find you a home." He put the dog in a wagon and pulled him to the McCurrys' house. Mark rang the doorbell.

"Hello," Mark said to Mrs. McCurry. "We are trying to give this dog away. Would you like to have him?"

"I'm afraid not. You see, we already have a dog and two cats. I don't think we need another animal around the house. Besides, even if we were getting a dog, I wouldn't want *that* one." With that she shut the door. Mrs. McCurry always was a blunt person.

"I guess we're out of luck there. How about the Gossets?" thought Mark to himself.

The radio was blaring loudly, and Mr. Gosset was outside washing his car. "Hello," he said. "What can I do for you?"

"Oh, I'm trying to give away this dog," Mark answered. "He doesn't have a home, and we don't want him to go to the pound. Would you take him?"

Mr. Gosset looked down at the ugly mutt and shook his head slowly from side to side. "No thanks," he said, and continued with his work.

Mrs. Perry was weeding her garden.

"Excuse me," Mark said.

"Yes?" Mrs. Perry asked. "What do you want?"

"Are you interested in having a dog?"

"Did you say a dog?" She gave a shrill whistle and seven puppies came bounding into the front yard.

"I'd best be going," Mark said.

Mark found his pals playing baseball on the vacant lot next door.

"Come on, Mark," one of them shouted. "You can be the pitcher."

"No thanks," Mark said. "I'll just watch."

Mark sat down on the curb, but his mind really wasn't on the game. He was thinking about Woof. His thoughts were soon interrupted when Barney hit a fly ball that bounced on the sidewalk and rolled into the middle of the street.

"I'll get it," Mark said, running toward the ball. But he did not see the minibus that came whizzing around the corner. The driver slammed on the brakes, but it was too late to stop. Mark screamed. The bus skidded into the direction of the frightened boy.

Seeing the danger, Woof made a dash for Mark and knocked him out of the way. But Woof didn't have enough time to save himself. The bus hit the back part of his body, and Woof skidded across the street, landing in the gutter.

Krissy and Mother heard the commotion and came running out of the house to see what had happened. Mark stumbled toward Woof. His tears fell on the street as he bent over the unconscious dog. Krissy ran back into the house to get an old blanket, and they wrapped it carefully around Woof's body. A neighbor carried him to the Petersons' porch and tried to keep him warm.

Mrs. Peterson hurriedly telephoned her husband to explain what had happened. Mr. Peterson soon arrived and put Woof in the back seat of their car. The family drove in silence to a local animal hospital.

Dr. Wilcox, the veterinarian, came out to the car and carried Woof into his inner office. Before closing the door, he said to Krissy and Mark, "I'll do the best I can."

The two children nodded appreciatively, but they were worried. Outside a storm was gathering. The thunder sounded like an echo of what was taking place inside Krissy's and Mark's pounding hearts. Their tears joined with the rain that had begun to fall.

Hours passed as they sat facing the big white door, waiting and waiting. Finally Krissy turned to Mark. "Maybe we should pray," she said.

"Yes," answered Mark.

They each closed their eyes and asked Jesus not to let the dog die. The big clock on the wall struck seven o'clock.

Finally the vet returned, closing the door behind him.

Mr. Peterson stood up. "How is he?"

"Well, your dog has a broken leg and some internal injuries. However, the damage is not serious enough to take his life. But I really believe Woof is dying. I just don't understand it. It's almost like he doesn't want to live." The veterinarian paused.

Krissy broke the silence. "I know why he doesn't want to live. He doesn't think he's loved. A dog needs love, just like people do."

"You're right about that," said the veterinarian.

"Doctor, can we see him?" asked Mark.

"Yes, of course, come on in," replied Dr. Wilcox.

They entered a small room where Woof lay on a table, whimpering softly. Krissy and Mark rushed to him. They gave him gentle hugs and stroked his rough fur. Mark then turned to his parents who were watching their children lovingly.

"Krissy is right," he said. "No wonder Woof doesn't want to get well, Dad. Maybe he knows he has no place to go. Maybe he understands he will be taken to the pound if he lives."

The corners of Mr. Peterson's mouth turned upward into a slight smile.

"How could I send a dog to the pound when he saved the life of my son? No sir! If this mutt lives, he is our dog for the rest of his life."

Krissy and Mark squealed with delight. Could it really be true? They laughed and jumped, thanking their mother and father. No one knew if Woof understood their happiness, but his little tail wagged just a bit as he rolled his big brown eyes toward them.

"Oh Woof!" said Krissy. "You just *have* to get well!"

"Let's go home and get some rest now," their father laughed, "or else we'll be spending time in a people hospital."

The next morning after breakfast the Petersons received a call from Dr. Wilcox. The children listened closely as their mother talked. After a short conversation, Mrs. Peterson hung up. Her face glowed as she said, "Woof is much better. Dr. Wilcox said we should be able to bring him home tomorrow afternoon."

The children had never been so excited. "Wait," Mrs. Peterson said firmly. "Didn't you ask God for something?" She then quoted a verse of Scripture from memory: "Don't worry about anything; instead, pray about everything; tell God your needs and don't forget to thank Him for his answers."

Krissy and Mark knelt down by the kitchen chairs and thanked the Lord for hearing their prayers and saving their dog. It really was a miracle!

The next afternoon when Mr. Peterson came home from work, the happy family went to the Small Animal Hospital. When they arrived, Woof seemed happy to see them. He was very sore and had a cast on his hind leg, but his tail was not injured. It thrashed back and forth vigorously.

That evening Krissy helped Mother cook dinner, and Mark sat down beside Woof, who was lying on his blanket. Neither of the children thought to ask what their father was doing in the garage or what was causing all the noise.

NUM-NUMS

NUTRIONALLY BALANCED

DOGS LOVE THIS NEW FOOD

After supper, when the children were ready for bed, Mr. Peterson picked up Woof and asked his family to come outside. There stood a beautiful redwood dog house. Above the door was a little sign that read:

WOOF

OUR SPECIAL HERO!